The House of Boo

BY

J. Patrick Lewis

ILLUSTRATED BY

Katya Krénina

Atheneum Books for Young Readers

Atheneum Books for Young Readers
An imprint of Simon & Schuster Children's
Publishing Division
1230 Avenue of the Americas
New York, New York 10020
Text copyright © 1998 by J. Patrick Lewis
Illustrations copyright © 1998 by Katya Krénina
All rights reserved including the right of reproduction
in whole or in part in any form.
Book design by Angela Carlino
The text of this book is set in Priska Serif.
The illustrations are rendered in gouache.
First Edition
Printed in Hong Kong
10 9 8 7 6 5 4 3 2 1
Library of Congress Cataloging-in-Publication Data
Lewis, J. Patrick.
The House of Boo / by J. Patrick Lewis ;
illustrated by Katya Krénina.—1st ed.
p. cm.
Summary: Three children visit the haunted house
of Boo Scoggins on Halloween and experience scary
sights and sounds.
ISBN 0-689-80356-7
[1. Haunted houses—Fiction. 2. Halloween—Fiction.
3. Stories in rhyme.] I. Krénina, Katya, ill. II. Title.
PZ8.3.L5855Ho   1998
[E]—dc21
97-16937
CIP   AC

To Lou, Cindy, and Clelia Rose

—J. P. L.

To my best friend, Rimma, with love

—K. K.

Boo Scoggins lived on Humpback Hill
Above the misty water mill.
His house was lit by pumpkin-light;
His songs were sung by whippoorwill.

Up from the river towns one night,
Three fearful children dressed in white
Came creeping toward the House of Boo—
Keeping carefully out of sight.

The sky had hung a moon so new
It cut fat pillow clouds in two.
Against the ancient house, a row
Of shutters clapped, the curtains blew.

As sudden bat wings angled low—
Three ghostly hearts were beating so—
A Shadow loomed across the stair,
Like something from a book by Poe!

The
crooked
fence
post
warned:

BEWARE!
Misfortune
follows
fools who dare.

Somewhere a cat unwound a whine
That gave the children such a scare

They flew like gossip from the sign!
In dark woods thick with creeper vine,
They tumbled down that vast surround
Of hill above the waterline.

The eerie hush was so profound
No screech owl dared disturb the sound-
Less night, and where dead leaves had blown,
Three children stumbled, homeward bound,

Upon a grisly cold headstone:

BOO
Scoggins
Lived
and
died
ALONE

As if to shake the night awake,
Wind wrapped itself around a moan.

A shovel lay beside a rake.
"Is this grave fresh?
It must be fake!"
"Boo's still alive.
Or is he . . . dead?"
They said, *"There must be some mistake!"*

Lights lit the town a mile ahead.
And though the children could have fled
Down the banks of the river glen,
They sat beside the grave instead—

Two river girls, a boy of ten—
And took a blood oath there and then:
*"Not one of us is staying here
If we climb up that hill again!"*

They overcame the hill of fear
To see the phantom reappear,
Imagining white-diamond eyes
Were watching them as they drew near.

Defiant as they reached the rise,
Each child threw off the ghost disguise
And snuck up to a windowsill
To catch Boo Scoggins by surprise!

Slant and gray in the bone-cold chill,
The haunted house on Humpback Hill
Was dark. Night huddled on the lawn.
A mournful call! The whippoorwill.

The doors were shut, the shades were drawn,
No pumpkin-lanterns flickered on.
A wizard wind unhinged the screen!
But Boo . . . and Shadow Boo . . . were gone.

What evening visitor had they seen?

Boo? Ghost? Or something in between?

It was too late to cry, *"WHO'S THERE?"*

To what it was . . . or might have been.

Three children took the double dare
That Halloween so long ago.

Deep in the bottomlands below,
The legend lives: Riverfolk know
The House of Boo grows cold and bare
On Humpback Hill, and still you'd swear
Someone is waiting . . .

                              waiting there,
Standing, watching . . . waiting there.

Author's Note

The House of Boo is a kind of poem called a Rubaiyat. Unlike most Rubaiyats ("Omar Khayyam," for example), this Halloween poem links the stanzas. That is, the third line's end word is the major rhyme in the following stanza—abba/bbcb/ccdc, etc. Robert Frost's "Stopping By Woods on a Snowy Evening" employs this same rhyme scheme.

—J. P. L.

DISCARDED

PEACHTREE

J PICTURE LEWIS   PTREE
Lewis, J. Patrick
The house of Boo

JUL 27 1999

Atlanta-Fulton Public Library